Holiday House / New York

For Jane and Nina

Printed and Bound in October 2014 at Tien Wah Press, Johor Bahru, Johor, Malaysia.
The artwork was created with watercolor and marker pen.
www.holidayhouse.com
First Edition
1 3 5 7 9 10 8 6 4 2

Library of Congress Cataloging-in-Publication Data
Schatell, Brian.
Owl boy / by Brian Schatell. — First edition.
pages cm
Summary: A boy likes owls and wishes only to do what owls do,
but will he really eat a mouse?
ISBN 978-0-8234-3208-0 (hardcover)
[1. Owls—Fiction.] I. Title.
PZ7.S3360w 2015
[E]—dc23
2014007383

When Al was two years old, he had a dream about owls.
It wasn't scary at all!

Now that he was older, all he thought about were . . .

owls.

IN FLIGHT
HOOTENANNY
NIGHT OWL
HOOT
OWL FACTS
1
2
3
4
5
6
WHOO-HOO-HOO
Hoot!
I HOOT 4 OWLS
THE OWL
EYE
WING
I ♥ OWLS
OWLS
POPULAR OWLS

OWLS
March of the
OWLS!
the MOVIE
coming to
a theater near you
OWL SIZE CHART
HOW
OWLS
FLY
1 2 3 4
5 6 7 8 9 10 11
12 13 14 15 16 17 18
19 20 21 22 23 24 25
26 27 28 29 30
OWL STORY
OWL
CHIPS
OWLS IN HISTORY
ALL ABOUT OWLS
HOOT!
OWL FACTS VOL 1
OWL MOON
OWL
OWLS
HOOT!
OWL SPOTTER GUIDE

He wasn't interested in much else.

Owls were about all that he liked.

"Why not call a friend?" said Al's mom.

"Why not play outside?" said his dad.

Al's older brother Fred liked football.
"Freddie," said Dad, "why not take Al along the next time you play with your friends?"
Freddie made Al play football, but Al was not very good at it.

Al's brother Ed liked basketball.
"Take Al with you, Eddie," said Mom.
"Do I have to?" said Eddie. He did.
Al did not excel at basketball.

Al's brother Ted liked baseball.
Al could not hit a ball.

Al didn't care much for school either, except when they studied owls. But that was only for one week, and Al already knew all the answers.

Once school was done for the year, Al's parents decided to send him to camp.

"Owls don't go to camp!" said Al.

"But you like birds . . . and trees and things," said his dad. "You'll love it!"

Reluctantly, Al went. . . .

He hated it.
For one thing, they served a lot of meat loaf.

Also, there were football teams, basketball teams, and baseball teams.

They had campfire sing-alongs.

It was "Everyone in your bunks by nine p.m.!"

One day Al and his bunk mates went on a hike.

TRAIL

Al decided to look for owl nests.

He got separated from the other campers.
Al was lost and alone.

It started to get dark.
"Boo-hoo-hoo," he cried.

"Whooo-hooo-hooooo," he heard!

Suddenly the moon came out and lit the woods.

An owl!

It was a dream come true!

Al and the owl explored. They hunted by moonlight.

The owl took him to secret places only owls knew about.

It was an owl extravaganza!

When it was over, Al felt a little hungry.
The owl flew off . . .

and returned with two mice.

It popped one in its mouth

and pushed the other toward Al.

YU

CK

The YUCK was so loud, the owl flew away.

The campers and counselors came running.

When Al got back to camp, he ate ten pieces of meat loaf.

He sang the loudest of any kid at the campfire.

That night he dreamed that he hit a home run . . .

and the next day he did!

When camp was over and Al went home,
he changed the pictures in his room.
He still liked owls, but let's face it . . .

. . . owls eat MICE!